Shaoey and Dot:
A Thunder and Lightning Bug Story

by **Mary Beth &
Steven Curtis Chapman**

Illustrated by Jim Chapman

NELSON

A Division of Thomas Nelson Publishers
Since 1798

www.thomasnelson.com

SHAOEY AND DOT: A THUNDER AND LIGHTNING BUG STORY

Published in Nashville, Tennessee, by Tommy Nelson®, a Division of Thomas Nelson, Inc.
Tommy Nelson® books may be purchased in bulk for educational, business, fundraising, or sales
promotional use. For information, please e-mail SpecialMarkets@ThomasNelson.com.

Library of Congress Cataloging-in-Publication Data

Chapman, Mary Beth.
  Shaoey and Dot : a thunder and lightning bug story / Mary Beth and Steven Curtis Chapman ; illustrated by Jim
Chapman.
     p. cm.
  Summary: When the lights go out during an electrical storm, Shaoey, a young Chinese American girl, is frightened
until Dot the ladybug reminds her of God's protection.
  ISBN 1-4003-0743-0
  [1. Fear of the dark—Fiction. 2. Christian life—Fiction. 3. Chinese Americans—Fiction. 4. Ladybugs—Fiction.
5. Stories in rhyme.] I. Chapman, Steven Curtis. II. Chapman, Jim, 1956– ill. III. Title.
PZ8.3.C3725Sf 2005
[E]—dc22
                                            2005030442

Printed in the United States of America
06 07 08 09 LBM 5 4 3 2 1

This book is dedicated to moms, dads, brothers, and sisters who have made room in their hearts for a child who didn't have a family.

It was cold. It was rainy. It was one of those nights
When the sky gets as dark as it gets.
Shaoey and Dot were enjoying a snack
Just before getting into their beds.

Suddenly there was a bright flash of light,
And the sky made a big, loud **ka-boom!**
Then as quick as the blink of a ladybug's eye,
All the light turned to dark in the room!

Shaoey's eyes widened to see nothing but dark,
And she called out to Dot, "Are you there?
Someone has turned out all of the lights!
I can't see you, and I'm getting scared!"

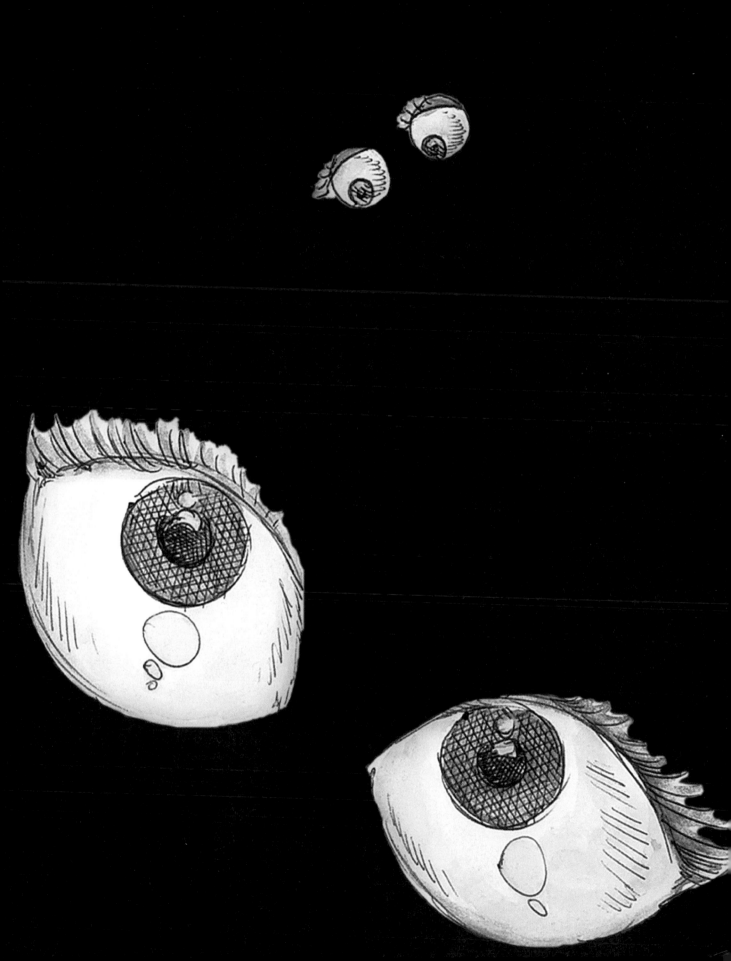

She waited and listened, and it felt like someone
Was beating a drum in her heart.
Then Dot said, "I'm here, and of all things to fear,
There's no need to be afraid of the dark."

"Now if you said a ten-foot-long alligator
Wanted you to help brush his teeth,
Or if maybe a whale was asleep in your bunk bed,
And you're in the one underneath . . ."

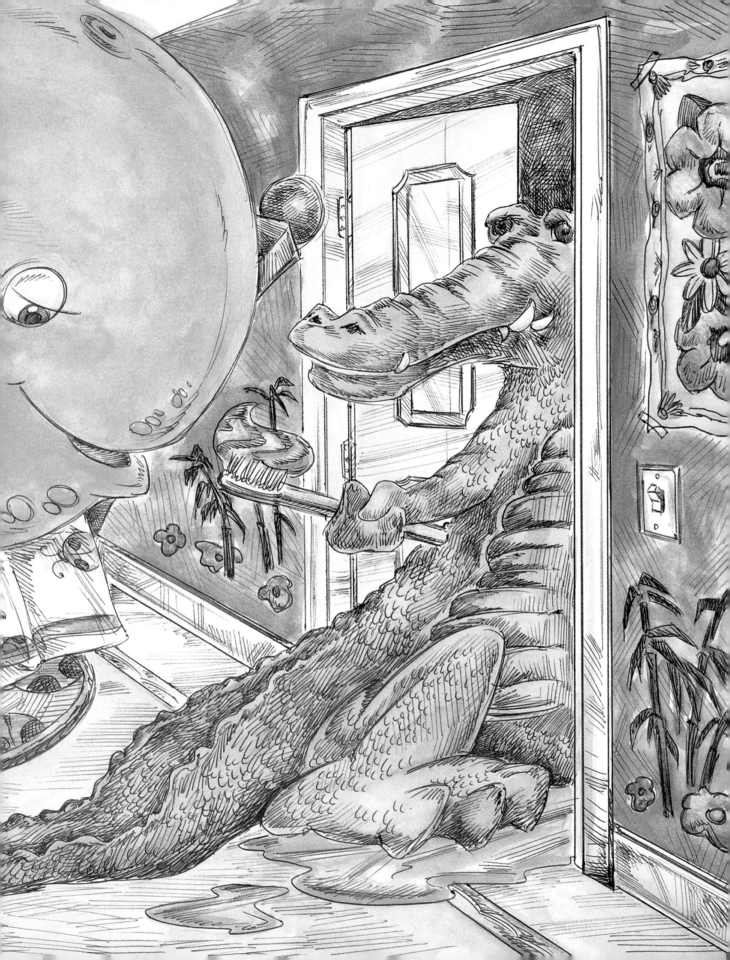

"Or if a whole family of hungry gorillas
Showed up at your door wanting lunch,
And all you could find was one rotten banana . . .
Well, that would scare me a whole bunch!"

"Or if you told me that
     you'd gone to the zoo,
And when you got back to your car,
A rhinoceros was waiting to ride home with you,
Then I think you'd have cause for alarm."

"But the dark's just a place with the lights out;
There's no reason to be afraid of it.
As a matter of fact, if you're a raccoon or a bat,
You'd probably say that you love it!"

"And even if you're a little girl or a bug,
There are *fun* things about the dark too.
It's a great place for sleeping and for hide-and-go-seeking—
And that's only naming a few!"

"But the one thing to always remember
Is that God's there, wherever you are.
He's always watching and taking care of you,
And His eyes even see in the dark!"

Then with a flash and a couple of flickers,
All the lights came back on in the room.
So they said their good-nights, then they
    turned off the lights,
And fell asleep by the glow of the moon.